Bertie's
BIG BLUE
Binoculars

Written by Keith Faulkner
Illustrated by Jo Davies

BARRON'S

It was Bertie's birthday! He was so excited as he sat on the floor with lots of brightly wrapped gifts piled high all around him.

At last there was only one gift left.

"Who's it from, Bertie?" asked Mom.

"Don't know. There's no label on it," he replied, expertly tearing off the paper to reveal a huge pair of bright blue binoculars.

"Cool! It's binoculars," he yelled excitedly.

Later that night as he stood in his bedroom, Bertie looked up into the starlit sky and saw the big, bright, shiny moon.

"Hmm! Now let's see how good these binoculars are," said Bertie to himself, as he pointed them skywards and peered through.

"Wow! They're magic binoculars!" exclaimed Bertie.

What was it that Bertie saw through the big blue binoculars? Why don't you look and see, too?

After looking out into space with his magic big blue binoculars for ages and ages, Bertie went to bed.

He lay there thinking what a great birthday it had been. He just couldn't wait until the morning so he could see what else the magic blue binoculars did.

Next morning, Bertie was having his breakfast. The big blue binoculars were around his neck. Then in from the garden came Wolf, Bertie's dog. Wolf's tongue was hanging out and his tail wagged. Bertie bent down to stroke him.

"Bertie! Go and wash your hands," said his mother. "Don't you know that dogs are covered with germs?"

Bertie washed his hands and came back to his breakfast.

"Germs . . . Huh! What germs?" muttered Bertie. But as he peered at Wolf through the big blue binoculars, he couldn't believe his eyes. Why don't you have a look, too?

When Bertie had finished breakfast, he went out into the garden to play with Wolf. First they played football, then Bertie threw some sticks for Wolf to fetch.

Suddenly a rabbit hopped across the grass and Wolf raced after it. Luckily for the rabbit, it reached its hole just in time and disappeared down inside, with Wolf barking and growling at the entrance.

Bertie ran to the rabbit hole and
crouched down to look in, but it was
too dark to see inside.

"I wonder what it's like down in a
rabbit hole . . . I know, I'll try my
magic binoculars," said Bertie,
peering through them down into the
dark rabbit hole.

Once again a look of complete
amazement came over Bertie's face.
What could he see through the big
blue binoculars? Why not have a
look for yourself?

Bertie was still looking at the amazing underground world, when he heard his mother call him.

"Bertie . . . Bertie, come and get ready. We're going out," she said.

"Out! Where to, Mom?" he asked.

"We're going out for a special birthday surprise."

It wasn't too long before Bertie discovered that they were going to the seaside and that Bertie's little brother Arthur was coming, too.

Bertie and Arthur had lots of fun at the seaside, building sandcastles, swimming in the sea, and climbing

on the rocks. They were having so much fun, in fact, that Bertie forgot all about his binoculars — for a while.

"Wow! Just have a look at this, Arthur," yelled Bertie, standing on a rock and looking down into the water with his magic binoculars.

Little Arthur looked through the binoculars and didn't believe his eyes. Bertie knew what he could see. Why don't you take a look?

"Get dressed now, boys," Mom said. "We have one more surprise before we go home."

And what a surprise it was! It was a visit to Bertie's very favorite place — the museum with the huge dinosaurs in it.

Bertie and Arthur stood and gazed in wonder at the enormous skeletons in the museum. All their favorite dinosaurs were there, including Bertie's very favorite dinosaur, the brontosaurus.

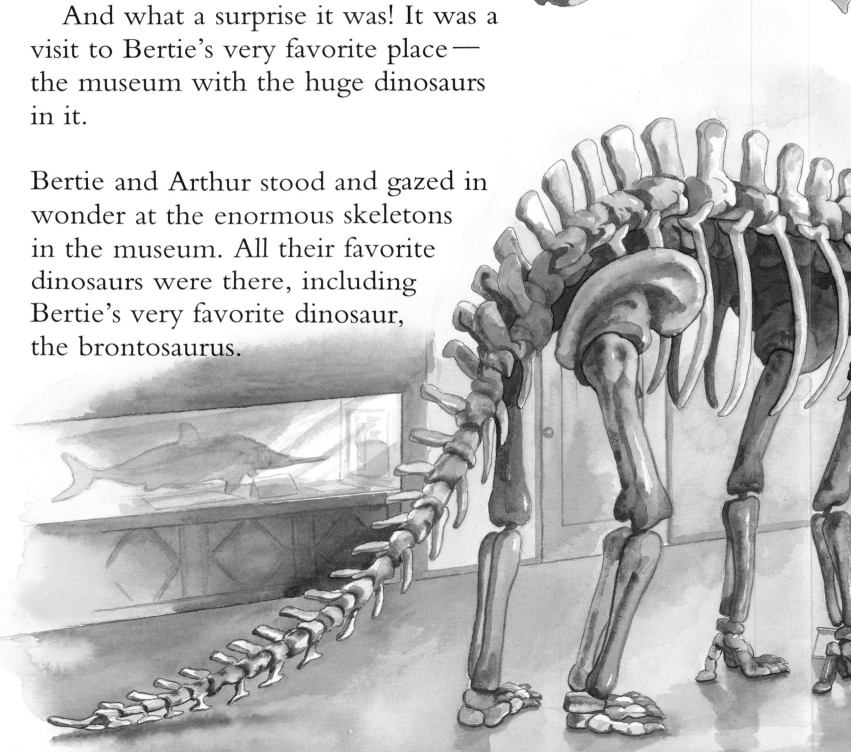

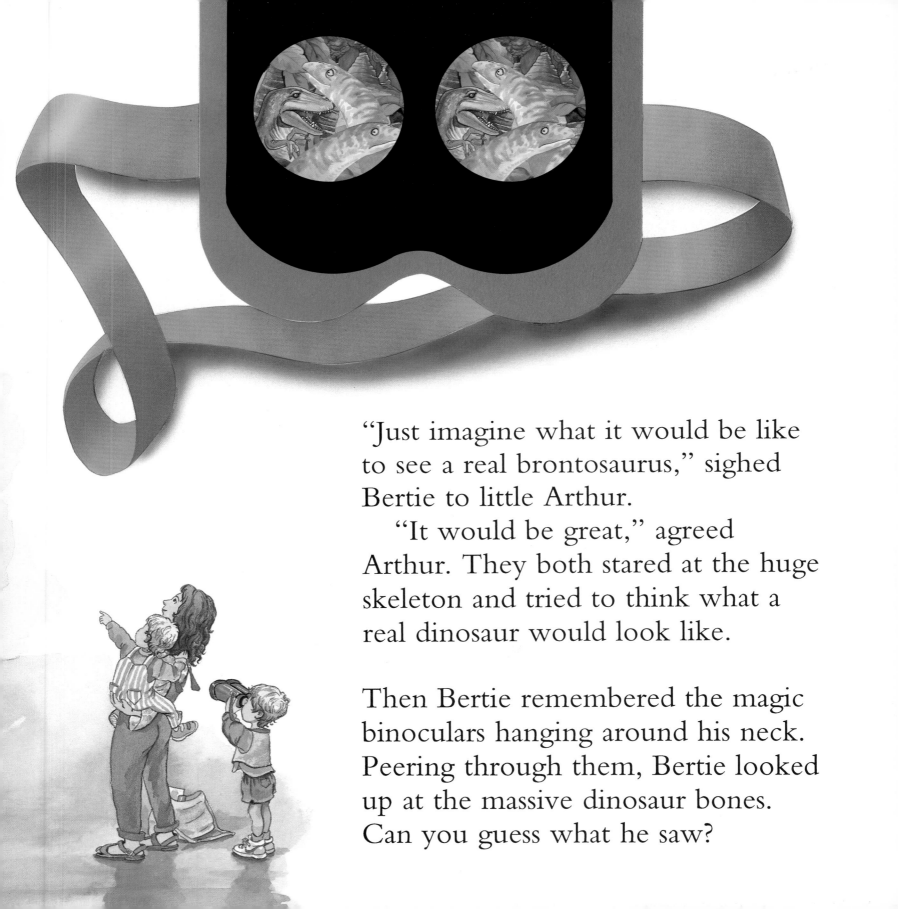

"Just imagine what it would be like to see a real brontosaurus," sighed Bertie to little Arthur.

"It would be great," agreed Arthur. They both stared at the huge skeleton and tried to think what a real dinosaur would look like.

Then Bertie remembered the magic binoculars hanging around his neck. Peering through them, Bertie looked up at the massive dinosaur bones. Can you guess what he saw?

Bertie and Arthur were tired out by the time they got home.

"Hop in the tub, you two and while you're in there, I'll get your supper ready," said Mom.

Bertie and Arthur had a big, bubbly bath and played with all their toys for a while. Then they put on their pajamas and bathrobes to go downstairs for supper.

"I'm really hungry," said little Arthur, rubbing his tummy. "Listen Bertie. My tummy is rumbling."

Bertie listened. Arthur was right.